Poké Rap

I want to be the very best there ever was
To beat all the rest, yeah, that's my cause

Catch 'em, Catch 'em, Gotta catch 'em all

Pokémon I'll search across the land
Look far and wide
Release from my hand
The power that's inside

Catch 'em, Catch 'em, Gotta catch 'em all
Pokémon!

Gotta catch 'em all, Gotta catch 'em all
Gotta catch 'em all, Gotta catch 'em all

At least one hundred and fifty or more to see
To be a Pokémon Master is my destiny

Catch 'em, Catch 'em, Gotta catch 'em all
Gotta catch 'em all, Pokémon! (repeat three times)

Can YOU Rap all 150?

Here's more of the Poké Rap
Catch book #8
Return of the Squirtle Squad
for the next 32 Pokémon!

Alakazam, Goldeen, Venonat, Machoke
Kangaskhan, Hypno, Electabuzz, Flareon
Blastoise, Poliwhirl, Oddish, Drowzee
Raichu, Nidoqueen, Bellsprout, Starmie

Metapod, Marowak, Kakuna, Clefairy
Dodrio, Seadra, Vileplume, Krabby
Lickitung, Tauros, Weedle, Nidoran
Machop, Shellder, Porygon, Hitmonchan

Words and Music by Tamara Loeffler and John Siegler
Copyright © 1999 Pikachu Music (BMI)
Worldwide rights for Pikachu Music administered by Cherry River Music Co. (BMI)
All Rights Reserved   Used by Permission

There are more books
about Pokémon.

Collect them all!

POKÉMON™

Splashdown in Cerulean City

Adapted by Tracey West

SCHOLASTIC INC.
New York   Toronto   London   Auckland   Sydney
Mexico City   New Delhi   Hong Kong

ISBN 0-439-15426-X

12 11 10 9 8 7 6   0 1 2 3 4 5 6/0

Printed in the U.S.A.

First Scholastic printing, March 2000

The World of Pokémon

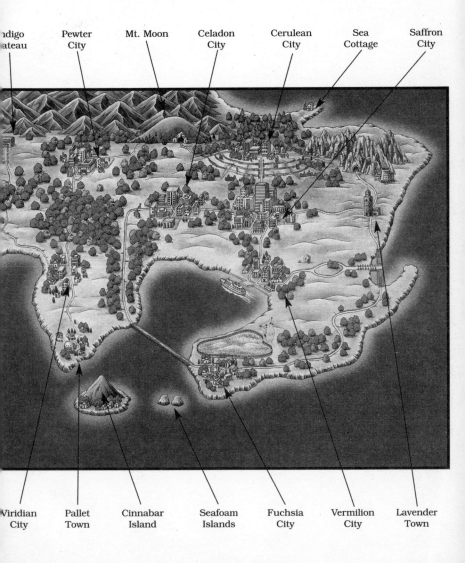

Indigo Plateau

Pewter City

Mt. Moon

Celadon City

Cerulean City

Sea Cottage

Saffron City

Viridian City

Pallet Town

Cinnabar Island

Seafoam Islands

Fuchsia City

Vermilion City

Lavender Town

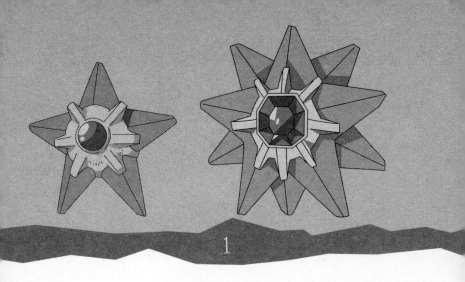

Misty's Secret

"Hurry up, Misty!" Ash Ketchum called out. "I'll never become a Pokémon Master at this rate. We've got to move fast if we want to keep up with the other Pokémon trainers."

"You can move as fast as you want, Ash," his friend Misty replied. "But it takes more than speed to become a Pokémon Master."

Ash spun around. His dark eyes flashed angrily. "What do you mean by that?" he asked.

"You know exactly what I mean!" Misty snapped.

Brock stepped between Ash and Misty.

"Stop all this arguing," Brock said. "Neither of you will learn how to take care of your Pokémon properly if you're always fighting."

Ash and Misty glared at each other without speaking a word. Brock looked at them both sternly.

The three friends were on a journey together — a journey to capture and train Pokémon, creatures with amazing powers.

Ten-year-old

Ash was a Pokémon trainer. He had started the journey with Pikachu — a bright yellow Pokémon that looked like a mouse. Pikachu had awesome electric powers. At first, Ash and Pikachu didn't get along. But now they were good friends.

Then Ash and Pikachu met Misty. This red-haired Pokémon trainer was on her own journey when she bumped into them. At first, Ash and Misty didn't get along — and they still didn't, sometimes.

Finally, they met Brock — a Gym Leader from Pewter City. Brock left his gym to learn how to become a great Pokémon breeder. Because Brock was a teenager and more experienced than Ash and Misty, he often gave them advice and helped them solve problems.

Like today. It seemed like Ash and Misty were always fighting.

"She started it," Ash protested.

Misty rolled her eyes. "That's so typical, Ash."

Brock sighed. "Can we go now?"

Ash pushed his red cap over his eyes. "Fine with me. I should be busy catching

Pokémon right now." He turned around and headed back down the dirt path. Pikachu followed at his heels.

Brock looked at Misty.

"Fine with me, too," she said.

Brock turned and walked away. But Misty lagged behind.

"Ash thinks he's so great," Misty muttered. She kicked at the dirt with her sneaker.

Ash is always talking about how he's going to be the world's greatest Pokémon Master, Misty thought. *He acts like he's the only Pokémon trainer in the world. But I'm a trainer, too.*

Misty thought about all of the Water Pokémon she had raised so carefully. Like Staryu, the mysterious Water

Pokémon that looked like a five-pointed starfish.

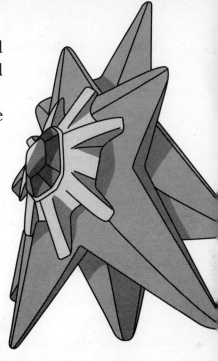

And Starmie, the evolved form of Staryu. Starmie was bigger than Staryu, with ten points instead of five. It could take a lot more damage in battle than Staryu. And Staryu's jewel was even more amazing than the one that glittered in the center of Starmie's body.

It's not easy to raise a Staryu and Starmie, Misty thought. *I bet Ash couldn't do it.*

Misty looked up at Ash — but he wasn't there.

"Oh, no!" Misty cried. Ash, Brock, and Pikachu were way ahead of her.

Misty ran down the trail. Her heavy knapsack bounced on her back.

"Wait for me!" Misty cried. She reached

her friends, puffing and panting.

"Where do you think you're going?" she asked.

"I know exactly where we're going," Ash replied. "We're going to Cerulean City."

Misty's heart skipped a beat.

Not Cerulean City. They couldn't go there. They just couldn't.

"What are you going there for?" she asked.

"Well, it's none of your business, but I'm going there to get a badge," Ash said. "If I battle the Gym Leader there and win, I'll earn a badge. You know I need badges from eight gyms to enter the Pokémon League."

Of course I know that, Misty thought. But there was no time to argue. She had to convince Ash not to go to Cerulean City.

"Uh, you don't want to battle over there," she said. "Trust me!"

Ash stopped and faced her. "Why not?"

"Because they have, uh, very scary Ghost Pokémon," she said. "They look like this!"

Misty stuck out her tongue and tried to make a scary face.

But Ash just laughed. "Nice face, Misty," he said. He turned to Brock and Pikachu. "Let's get going!"

Misty ran in front of Ash and blocked his way. "How about Vermilion City? It's right on the water, and there are lots of Pokémon there, and —"

"We're going to Cerulean City!" Ash insisted. "I've got to get that badge."

"It makes sense to me," Brock said.

Ash gave Misty a triumphant look. "Then let's go already!"

Misty sighed as Ash, Brock, and Pikachu headed down the trail to Cerulean City.

Once we get there, they'll find out my secret, Misty thought. *And then what will I do?*

While Misty and her friends walked to Cerulean City, three other Pokémon trainers were already there — and causing trouble.

It was Team Rocket, of course. Jessie, James, and their Pokémon, Meowth, were a trio of Pokémon thieves. If they saw a chance to steal Pokémon, they'd take it.

And now they had a plan.

The three thieves broke into a warehouse. A large metal machine loomed in front of them.

"A giant vacuum!" Jessie said. "It's perfect."

"And there's a giant hose," James said. He pointed to a big tube that looked wide enough to fit a person inside.

"*Meowth!* This is too good to be true," said the catlike Pokémon.

"But it *is* true," said Jessie, her gray eyes gleaming. "We've got what we need. And when we're through —"

"Cerulean City will never be the same!" James finished.

The Cerulean City Gym

Misty, Ash, Brock, and Pikachu didn't have far to walk before the gates to Cerulean City rose in front of them.

"Good luck at the gym," Brock said. "I'll catch up with you later. I've got to shop for more Pokémon food ingredients. I'm out."

"I've got some stuff to take care of, too," Misty said.

"Where are you going?" Ash asked, but Misty didn't reply. She ducked down a side street.

Misty walked down the tree-lined street, sulking.

She couldn't face Ash and Brock. Not yet.

Misty turned a corner. In the distance, she could see the Cerulean City Gym.

The large, round building looked almost like a carousel. Orange and pink pillars held up a domed roof. On the roof in front of the gym was a giant statue of a Seel. This Water Pokémon looked like a white seal.

Misty looked at the gym. Part of her longed to go inside.

But I shouldn't go, Misty thought. *If I just stay away until Ash gets his badge, he won't find out my secret.*

CERULEAN GYM

But Misty walked a little closer. The sound of music and people cheering floated out of the gym.

Misty couldn't resist.

I'll hide in the crowd, she thought. *No one will see me.*

So Misty walked through the gym doors. Inside, the gym looked like a stadium. Rows of seats circled a large swimming pool shaped like a rectangle. The seats were filled with people.

Misty found a seat in the very top row. Then the gym lights dimmed.

An announcer's voice blared over loudspeakers, "Ladies and gentlemen, please welcome the stars of our show: the Sensational Cerulean City Synchronized Swimming Sisters!"

A spotlight shone on a diving board high above the pool. Three teenage girls in bathing suits stood on the board. They all looked sort of alike, but one had blue hair, one had pink hair, and the third had blond hair.

"Give a cheer for Violet, Lily, and Daisy!" the announcer cried.

The girls smiled and waved to the crowd. Then one by one, they dove into the water.

For almost an hour, the girls swam and did tricks in the water. Misty yawned through most of it.

Finally, the show was over. The crowd filed out of the stadium.

Misty stayed back, hidden behind a pillar.

She looked down at the pool. Lily, Violet, and Daisy had climbed out of the pool and were drying off. Someone was approaching them. A boy and a Pokémon.

Ash and Pikachu!

Misty stayed hidden and listened carefully.

"Uh, excuse me," Ash said.

Lily, the pink-haired girl, looked annoyed. "We don't do autographs," she said.

"I don't want one," Ash said. "I just want to know if this is a Pokémon gym."

"It sure is!" said Daisy, the blond.

"Well, I'm looking for the Gym Leader," Ash said.

Violet, the blue-haired girl, smiled. "You're looking at them!"

Ash looked stunned. "Huh?"

"The three of us are the Gym Leaders here," Daisy said.

"Gym Leaders?" Ash asked. "But what's with all that swimming?"

"It's, like, our hobby," Lily explained. "We call ourselves the Sensational Sisters. Our fans love to watch us perform."

"We *pool* our talents to make a big *splash!*" Violet said.

The three sisters burst into laughter.

Ash looked even more annoyed than ever. He took a Poké Ball from his belt.

"Come on!" he said, holding the Poké Ball in the air. "I challenge all of you!"

Pikachu stood next to Ash, ready to battle. *"Pika!"* Pikachu cried.

The sisters frowned.

"We don't feel much like battling anymore," Daisy said.

"We were just beaten three times in a row by kids from this nowhere place called Pallet Town," Violet explained. "It was just one defeat after another."

From her hiding place, Misty chuckled quietly. Ash was from Pallet Town, too. The other trainers were always ahead of him.

"We had to practically, like, rush all of our Pokémon to the Pokémon Center," Daisy said.

Lily held up a Poké Ball and threw it. "This is the only one we have left."

Goldeen, a Water Pokémon that looked like a frilly goldfish, appeared in a flash of light.

"You mean that's the only Pokémon you have?" Ash asked.

Daisy shrugged. "So, like, there's no point in battling," she said.

That's a relief, Misty thought. Now we can get out of here.

Ash looked crushed.

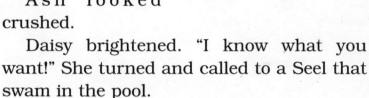

Daisy brightened. "I know what you want!" She turned and called to a Seel that swam in the pool.

"Seel, come here!" Daisy said.

Seel hopped out of the pool. It slid along the floor to Daisy's side. Then it opened its mouth. A blue badge glittered there.

Daisy took the badge from Seel and offered it to Ash. "This is what you came here for," she said. "Just take it."

Misty couldn't believe it. She watched the group angrily. It wasn't fair. Ash should have to earn his badge, like everyone else.

"Uh, I'd rather win the badge in a battle," Ash said. But Daisy pressed it into his hand. "Take it," she said. "A badge is a badge."

"Well, okay," Ash said hesitantly. Then he smiled at the badge in his hand.

It was too much for Misty. She jumped out from behind the pillar and ran down the stadium aisle.

"Hold it right there!" she cried.

The three sisters and Ash all stared at Misty.

"What are you doing here?" Ash asked.

Misty ignored him. "Daisy, if you don't want to battle him, I will!"

"What are you talking about?" Ash asked.

"I'm a Cerulean City Gym Leader, too," Misty said. "I'm the fourth Sensational Sister!"

3

Ash vs. Misty

"You're the fourth Sensational Sister?" Ash asked in disbelief.

Lily snickered. "You mean three Sensational Sisters — and one runt!"

"So, little sister," Daisy said. "It's a surprise to see you back so soon."

"That little girl with the big mouth who said she wouldn't come back until she was a great Pokémon trainer — wasn't that you?" Violet asked.

The three sisters circled Misty. Misty felt angry and embarrassed at the same time.

She didn't want to come back until she had something to show off to her sisters. Something to make them proud.

And right now she didn't have too much — except an annoying friend named Ash.

"So *that's* why you were so dead set against coming here," Ash said.

Lily laughed. "Face it, Misty. The only reason you left here to become a Pokémon trainer is because you couldn't compare with us," she said. "We're *obviously* much more talented and beautiful than you are!"

"That wasn't the reason!" Misty said angrily. "I'm a good Pokémon trainer. I just left to get more experience."

"Then why are you back so soon?" Violet asked. "I guess you couldn't make it as a trainer after all."

"That's not true!" Misty cried. "It wasn't my idea to come back here. It was *his*." She pointed to Ash.

Daisy eyed Ash. "Well, he's totally not someone I'd choose for a boyfriend, but you're no prize yourself."

Ash made a face. And Misty exploded.

"Boyfriend! He's not my boyfriend!" Misty yelled. "If I battle him, it'll prove I'm not a quitter and I'm just as good a trainer as you three."

Daisy sighed. "You might as well. You're the only one of us with Pokémon that can actually battle."

Misty faced Ash. "If you want that Cascade Badge, you'll have to beat me first!"

"It'll be my pleasure!" Ash said.

"Fine," Misty said. "In this gym, the battle area is the pool."

Misty climbed onto a red raft on one end of the pool — the Gym Leader's platform.

Ash climbed onto a blue raft — the challenger's platform. Pikachu stood next to him.

Misty held up a Poké Ball. "We can each use two Pokémon," Misty said. "Let the battle begin!"

Ash picked up Pikachu. "Pikachu, I choose you!" He tried to throw Pikachu into the pool.

But Pikachu clung to Ash's neck. The yellow lightning mouse looked sad and pointed at Misty.

"*Chuu chuu,*" Pikachu said.

Ash understood Pikachu's language. "Are you saying you don't want to battle with Misty?" Ash asked.

Pikachu nodded. "*Pikachu,*" it said.

"I guess it's okay if you don't want to battle a friend," Ash said reluctantly.

"Pikachu, you're a pika pal!" Misty called out.

Pikachu smiled.

But Ash didn't look happy. "Too bad, Pikachu. You'd do great against Misty's Water Pokémon."

Ash threw a Poké Ball out over the pool. "Butterfree! I choose you!"

A bright light flashed. Butterfree flew out of the ball. The Flying Pokémon looked like a large butterfly.

Misty felt confident.

"Misty calls Staryu!" she cried. She tossed a Poké Ball into the air.

Staryu burst out of the ball. It stood on two of its points at the edge of the platform.

Ash looked bewildered. He had never seen a Staryu before.

"What is it?" Ash wondered aloud. He took out his Pokédex, a handheld computer with information about all kinds of Pokémon.

"Staryu," the Pokédex said. "The core of this Water Pokémon shines in a rainbow of seven colors. The core is valued by some as a type of jewelry."

"Leave it to a girl to show off her jewelry!" Ash teased.

"Quit stalling!" Misty snapped. "Let's battle!"

The smile faded from Ash's face. "Butterfree, you can blow this thing away with one blast. Tackle it!" Ash commanded.

Butterfree flew straight at Staryu and knocked it down.

"Staryu, counterattack!" Misty cried.

Staryu jumped up. It began to spin around. Then it took off into the air, like a flying machine.

Staryu aimed right for Butterfree.

"Butterfree, Dodge!" Ash ordered.

The Flying Pokémon dodged Staryu's attack.

Ash laughed. "This is so easy. I'm going to win."

"Don't count on it!" Misty said. "Staryu, Water Gun!"

In a flash, Staryu jumped into the water. It popped back onto the platform. A forceful stream of water shot out of Staryu's top point.

Butterfree quickly dodged the Water Attack.

"Butterfree, Stun Spore now!" Ash countered.

Butterfree flapped its wings. Shimmering yellow particles poured from its body. They  floated through the air and covered Staryu.

"Oh, no!" Misty cried. "Staryu looks like it's in real pain!"

"How can you tell?" Ash asked. "It doesn't even have a face!"

"Because I'm sensitive to others' feelings, that's how!" Misty snapped. "Staryu, wash it off!"

Staryu quickly jumped into the pool and dove deep into the water. When it jumped back out, the Stun Spores were gone.

Ash wasn't discouraged. "Butterfree, Sleep Powder!" he cried.

Butterfree slapped its wings again, and this time, silver particles filled the air.

But Staryu was ready. It jumped into the water before the powder could hit it.

Then suddenly, without warning, Staryu jumped out of the pool. It crashed into Butterfree. The Flying Pokémon fell into the pool. It helplessly flapped its wings in the water.

Misty cheered. Staryu had done it! Butterfree couldn't battle anymore.

From the sidelines, Misty's sisters watched the battle.

"Misty's, like, totally awesome," Daisy remarked in disbelief.

Lily shrugged. "Well, we three got the good looks in the family. I guess she had to get *some* talent!"

Ash looked angry. He threw another Poké Ball.

"Pidgeotto, I choose you!" he yelled.

Misty thought fast. Pidgeotto was a Flying Pokémon, too. It looked like a bird. But Pidgeotto was a little more powerful than Butterfree.

She knew what to do.

"Staryu, return!" she called. She threw a Poké Ball in the air. "Misty calls Starmie!"

Ash grimaced at the sight of the stronger Pokémon.

"Pidgeotto, Whirlwind it away!" he commanded.

Pidgeotto furiously flapped its wings. The movement created a spinning wheel of air. The whirlwind rolled toward Starmie.

"Dive under, then up!" Misty told her Pokémon.

Starmie jumped into the pool just in time. It popped up again a few seconds later, aimed right for Pidgeotto.

"Strike back with Wing Attack!" Ash ordered Pidgeotto.

Pidgeotto used one of its powerful wings to knock down Starmie before Starmie could hit it. The Water Pokémon plunged into the pool.

Starmie leaped out of the water again. But once again, Pidgeotto knocked it back into the pool.

"Now use Gust to blow it away!" Ash cried.

Starmie jumped into the air. Pidgeotto flapped its wings. A forceful gust of wind pushed Starmie through the air. Starmie crashed into the gym doors. Then it sank to the floor.

Misty gasped. The jewel in Starmie's

center usually glowed with a red light. But the light was fading.

"Starmie's energy is about to run out!" she cried. This was terrible. If Starmie lost its energy, Ash would win the battle.

And her sisters would never respect her.

"Come on, Starmie!" Misty called out. "You can do it!"

Then a strange noise made her spin around. It sounded like stone cracking.

Misty looked. One of the gym walls *was* cracking.

The wall began to crumble before Misty's eyes.

Suddenly, a large machine crashed through the wall. It was a large silver machine with a big hose attached to it.

And riding on the machine was Team Rocket — Jessie, James, and Meowth!

"Like, who invited the party crashers?" Daisy asked.

Jessie sneered. "Sorry to break in on you ladies . . ." she began.

James finished the threat. " . . . but we've got some Water Pokémon to steal!"

4

Team Rocket's Plan

"Water Pokémon have an advantage in water," James said.

"But if we steal that water away . . ." said Jessie.

" . . . the Pokémon are ours for the taking!" Meowth finished. With that, the catlike Pokémon flipped a switch on the giant machine.

Misty watched, stunned, as a giant tube emerged from the machine. The tube snaked into the pool and started sucking out the water.

Misty gasped when she realized what was happening. The machine was a giant vacuum. Team Rocket was sucking the water out of the pool!

Misty turned to her sisters. "We've got to stop them! With that vacuum, they'll be able to capture our Water Pokémon."

Lily faced Meowth. "Hey! Like, that's our water!" she yelled.

Meowth smiled. "Right," it said. "I should give it back."

Meowth flipped another switch. The hose lifted out of the water. Then a hard spray of water shot out and hit Ash, Misty, and her sisters.

It knocked them right out!

Team Rocket laughed. Meowth put the hose back in the water and turned up the power. The hose sucked up the pool water — and more.

The hose caught Goldeen first. The sisters' Pokémon disappeared up the tube and into the vacuum tank.

Seel, the gym mascot, was sucked in next.

31

Stunned from the water blast, Misty opened her eyes just in time to see the white Water Pokémon in Team Rocket's clutches.

"Seel! Come back!" Misty's sisters called out.

"Pikachuuu!"

It was Pikachu. The Pokémon had fallen into the pool. Team Rocket's hose was about to suck it up.

"Pikachu! We've got you at last!" James cried.

Ash looked panicked. "Pikachu! No!" he yelled.

Then Ash's face lit up.

"I've got it!" he said. "Water conducts electricity. Pikachu, Thunderbolt!"

"Pika!" Tiny sparks flew from Pikachu's red cheeks. Pikachu concentrated with all its might. Then it let loose with a massive charge of electricity.

The crackling energy traveled up the stream of water, into the hose, and electrified the giant metal vacuum.

Jessie, James, and Meowth screamed as

the electricity shocked them. The force of
the energy sent them flying off the vacuum,
out the hole in the wall, and up into the
sky.

"Look's like Team Rocket's blasting off
again!" they cried.

"Way to go, Pikachu!" Ash said.

But the vacuum was still on. Misty and
the others watched helplessly as the hose
finished the job and sucked Pikachu into
the vacuum.

"Like, this is terrible!" Violet said.

"No problem!" Ash said. He ran to the vacuum and flipped a switch. The hose spit all of the water back into the pool. Then Goldeen, Seel, and Pikachu poured out. They were all safe.

"Ash, you're, like, so cool!" the three sisters said.

Misty rolled her eyes. *What a show-off he is,* she thought. She turned to Ash. "Hey, we never got to finish our match!" she said.

"Yeah, and I was just about to win," Ash said.

"What do you mean?" Misty asked angrily.

Violet stepped between them. "You could say that your match had to be postponed, like, due to *drain.*"

"At least nobody lost," Lily added.

"But I wanted to win," Misty protested.

"And I wanted to get that Cascade Badge," Ash said. He looked down at his sneakers. "I guess I'll never get it now."

Daisy smiled. "Wrong. We're giving the badge to you," she said. She handed him the blue gem.

Misty couldn't believe it. "How come he gets the badge? He didn't win," she said.

"Pikachu was the one that, like, totally saved us all," Daisy said. "If Ash had used Pikachu from the start, there was no way your Water Pokémon could have won."

Misty sighed. Deep down, she knew her sisters were probably right. But she had wanted to win that match so badly, to prove she was a great Pokémon trainer.

Lily noticed her frown. "Misty, keep trying to be a Pokémon trainer. You might as well be good at *something*. After all, you'll never be stars like us."

"Keep that up and you'll be *seeing* stars!" Misty threatened. She wished her sisters would quit picking on her.

"Chill out," Violet said.

"You know we love you," said Daisy.

"Yeah," Misty replied.

She knew her big sisters loved her.

But would they ever respect her?

5

The Princess Festival

After Ash earned his Cascade Badge, the friends continued their Pokémon journey.

Misty made a vow to become a great Pokémon trainer — someone her sisters would look up to. She tried to catch and train as many new Pokémon as she could.

She caught Horsea, a Water Pokémon that looked like a blue seahorse.

She found Psyduck, a Water Pokémon that looked like a yellow duck. At first, Misty thought she had made a big mistake when she caught Psyduck. The Pokémon was weak in battle, and usually ended up making a mess of Misty's strategies. Then Misty discovered that Psyduck had an amazing Psychic Attack called Confusion. If Psyduck got a headache, it could use its Confusion Attack to make its opponent confused and dizzy. That attack earned Psyduck a victory almost every time.

Misty was also taking care of Togepi, a rare Pokémon that hatched from an egg Ash had found. When Togepi hatched, Misty was the first person it saw, and the little Pokémon bonded with her. Togepi's head, arms, and legs stuck out of its shell. Misty usually carried the Pokémon in her arms, or in her knapsack.

Thanks to all of her new Pokémon, Misty was in a pretty good mood. And when she, Ash, Brock, and Pikachu stumbled upon the Princess Festival, she was even more thrilled.

"This is great!" Misty said as they walked down a busy street. "I love the Princess Festival."

The street was crowded with girls and

women of all ages. The shops along the street were packed. Music filled the air, and fireworks sparkled in the daylight sky.

"Of course you love the Princess Festival," Ash complained. "You're a girl. Girls get tons of free food and stuff. And discounts at all the stores. But what do us guys get? Nothing. It's not fair."

Misty grinned. The Princess Festival was great. But seeing Ash jealous was a bonus.

"It's only one day a year, Ash," Misty said. "Can't you stand it for just one day?"

Ash kicked the pavement. "Ah, I don't know. Maybe Brock and I will go somewhere else today. Right, Brock?"

Brock didn't answer. He was too busy staring at a pretty girl who walked by.

"Brock? Did you hear me?" Ash asked.

Brock didn't take his eyes off the girl. "I love the Princess Festival," he said in a voice like a zombie.

Ash sighed. "I guess we'll stay with you."

"Great!" Misty said. "Let's go shopping."

Misty pushed her way through the crowd. A few doors down, she saw a sign that read BIG SALE TODAY!

A crowd of people filled the entrance to the store. Misty squeezed inside.

Clothes were piled in huge heaps on sale tables. Misty saw a cool blue shirt sticking out from one of the piles. She reached out and grabbed it.

Someone else grabbed it, too.

It was Jessie, from Team Rocket!

"Not you again!" Misty said.

"Let go of it, you little twerp," Jessie said.

"You let go," Misty protested. "I saw it first!"

Jessie glared at Misty. "I know how we can settle this. Let's have a battle to decide!"

"Fine with me!" Misty said. She dropped the shirt and took a Poké Ball from her knapsack.

Jessie dropped the shirt and picked up a Poké Ball, too.

Another girl walked by and grabbed the shirt.

"Hey!" Misty and Jessie cried.

Then a voice on a loudspeaker filled the air.

"Attention, Princess Festival shoppers," the announcer said. "In just a few minutes

in our auditorium, we will be holding the main event of this year's Princess Festival — the Queen of the Princess Festival Contest."

The crowd went silent. Everyone wanted to hear about the contest.

"The prize for the contest winner will be a beautiful, one-of-a-kind collection of Pokémon Princess dolls," the announcer said.

"Princess dolls!" Misty and Jessie said together.

The two girls looked at each other.

"Say, kid," Jessie said. "Why don't we use the contest to resolve our little dispute?"

"And the winner gets to keep the doll collection?" Misty asked.

Jessie nodded.

"Then it's settled," Misty said. "We'll both enter the contest. But I'll be the one to win!"

6

Princess vs. Princess

Misty and Jessie rushed to the contest headquarters. As soon as they signed up they were whisked into dressing rooms. Several women fussed over Misty. They brushed out her ponytail so her red hair gleamed on her shoulders. They gave her a fancy kimono to wear — a long silk robe decorated with flowers and butterflies. Then they whisked her to an open-air stage.

Misty lined up with the other contestants. Jessie stood next to her. She was dressed up in a kimono, too.

Misty looked out at the crowd. She couldn't believe she was actually in the contest. It was all happening so fast.

Misty spotted Ash, Pikachu, and Brock in the crowd. She waved.

Ash's face lit up in surprise. He didn't recognize her!

A man in a suit walked out onto the stage. He was the emcee, or announcer.

"We have quite a competition this year," said the emcee. "The winner of our contest must be as poised as a Jynx, sit as serene-

ly as a Jigglypuff, and possess the grace and charm of an Oddish."

The crowd applauded.

"I shouldn't have any problem winning this," Misty whispered to Jessie.

"Oh, I'm sure you'll win the contest, little girl," Jessie said snidely. "That is, if they have a peewee division."

Misty wanted to stick out her tongue, but she kept still. She didn't want to ruin her chances with the judges.

The emcee continued. "And now let's all take a look at the special prize they'll be competing for!" He waved his arm, and a curtain lifted next to him. Behind the curtain was a set of dolls. Pikachu, Clefary, Squirtle, Bulbasaur, Charmander, Jynx, Jigglypuff, Chansey, Polywhirl, and Slowbro dolls were all dressed up in fancy clothes.

"There's no other set like it in the world!" said the emcee. "It's unique! It's antique! It's a beautiful, handmade, custom-crafted, one-of-a-kind, luxury Pokémon Princess doll set! Batteries not included."

44

"Pokémon Princess dolls," Misty said breathlessly.

"The only set in the world," Jessie said.

The girls stared at each other.

Jessie sneered. "You're sure putting a lot of effort into a contest you're going to lose, aren't you?" she asked.

"We'll see who loses," Misty said.

The emcee interrupted them. "Now would all contestants please prepare their Poké Balls?"

"You mean you want us to battle?" Misty asked.

"This isn't just a beauty contest?" asked Jessie.

"Oh, no," replied the emcee. "The Festival contest winner also has to be a skilled Pokémon trainer!"

The emcee waved his hand, and another curtain rose. Behind it was a large chart showing all of the contestants. They were divided into two groups. Misty saw that she and Jessie were in different groups.

"The contestants are broken up into two divisions, the Eastern Division and the Western Division," the emcee said. "The two winners from each division will battle each other. The winner of that battle will be crowned Queen of the Princess Festival."

"Each contestant may use up to four Pokémon to battle," the emcee continued. "Now, let the competition begin!"

The crowd clapped and cheered. Misty, Jessie, and the other contestants were ushered offstage.

Misty quickly changed into her own clothes and put her hair back in its ponytail. Then she ran out to meet Ash, Brock, and Pikachu.

"Please, guys," she said when she saw them. "I need to borrow your Pokémon, just for the contest. My Water Pokémon are strong, but I need different Types of Pokémon if I'm going to win this."

"That's true," Brock said. "It's important to have a balance of Pokémon Types."

"Right," Ash agreed. "But our Pokémon won't just listen to any trainer, you know."

"If you tell them to obey all my instructions they will," Misty pleaded. "Please say yes!"

Ash hesitated. But Pikachu smiled. The yellow Pokémon jumped into Misty's arms and hugged her.

"Thanks, Pikachu," Misty said.

Ash shook his head. "You must really want to beat Jessie."

Misty paused. "I'm doing it for the doll set," she said.

"The doll set?" Ash asked.

"You're an only child. You wouldn't understand," Misty began. "But when you're the youngest of four sisters, having something that belongs to you, only you, is important.

"My sisters all had their own Princess dolls," Misty continued. "All I ever got was their broken old hand-me-downs. But now I'll win my very own set of Pokémon Princess dolls!"

And show my sisters that I'm just as good as they are, Misty added silently.

Brock shrugged. "It must be a girl thing."

"Or maybe it's just a *Misty* thing," Ash cracked.

Misty glared at him.

"Calm down," Brock said. "We'll help. You can borrow our Pokémon so you'll have a strong, well-balanced team."

"Yeah," Ash said reluctantly. "We'll help."

48

The three friends walked over to a park bench and began to plan Misty's strategy. Soon Misty's team of Pokémon stood before her.

"Pikachu is an Electric Type," Misty said, looking at the group of Pokémon. "Ash's Bulbasaur is a Grass Type. Brock's Vulpix is a Fire Type. And with my Starmie as a Water Type, how can I lose?"

She turned to Brock and Ash. "Thanks for your help, guys."

Ash knelt down and talked to Pikachu and Bulbasaur. "You two do whatever Misty tells you to do. Now go out there and win!"

"You too, Vulpix," Brock added. He petted the Fire Pokémon, which looked like a fox.

"Thanks, all of you," Misty said. "Now I'm ready to battle!"

Soon Misty stood in the Princess Festival stadium, facing her first opponent.

The brown-haired girl looked like she was Misty's age. She stood before Misty with a determined look on her face.

A bell rang. The girl threw a Poké Ball into the air.

"Go, Kingler!" she cried.

There was a flash of light. Then Kingler appeared. This Water Pokémon looked like a large crab with sharp claws.

Misty knew it was a tough opponent. But she also knew how to beat it.

"Go, Bulbasaur!" she cried.

Misty threw Bulbasaur's Poké Ball. The combination Plant and Poison Pokémon burst out of its Poké Ball in a shock of light. It looked like a dinosaur with a plant bulb on its back.

"Bulbasaur, Vine Whip!" Misty commanded.

Bulbasaur obeyed Misty's order. The plant bulb on its back opened up. Two green vines shot out.

The vines lunged through the air. They wrapped around Kingler's claws. Then the vines lifted Kingler up and pounded the Water Pokémon into the ground.

"The attack against Kingler has worked," the announcer said. "Kingler's been Vine Whipped and the poor Pokémon is powerless!"

Misty's opponent frowned. She recalled Kingler and sent out Rattata.

Rattata looked like a rat with sharp teeth. It charged at Bulbasaur.

"Bulbasaur, Razor Leaf!" Misty cried.

Sharp leaves flew from Bulbasaur's plant bulb. The leaves attacked Rattata. The Normal Pokémon couldn't fight them off, and quickly fainted.

"Two down, two to go!"

Misty's opponent sent out Cubone next. This strange Ground Pokémon wore a mask of bone and carried a club.

Bulbasaur easily defeated Cubone with Vine Whip.

Next, the other trainer called on Pinsir, a powerful Bug Pokémon.

But Bulbasaur was better. Another Razor Leaf Attack took out Pinsir in a flash.

"Misty wins the first round!" cried the announcer.

"And I'm going to have a very strong finish, too," Misty vowed.

Misty went on to face the next opponent in her division. And the next.

Thanks to Pikachu, Bulbasaur, Vulpix, and Starmie, Misty beat her opponents one by one.

"With a whole variety of Pokémon, young Misty from the Eastern Division has won a spot in the finals!" the announcer said.

Excited, Misty ran to Ash and Brock in the stands.

"I'm going to win this thing!" she said. "I'm going to get that doll set."

"You've been handling the Pokémon really well," Brock said.

"Yeah," Ash admitted. "You're pretty good."

"Thanks," Misty said. "And now I've just got one more opponent to beat."

"And now let's welcome Misty's opponent to the stadium," the announcer said. "From the Western Division, it's Jessie!"

Misty gasped. Jessie walked out onto the field, dressed in her Team Rocket uniform.

"Those Princess dolls are mine!" Jessie said.

"We'll see about that!" Misty replied.

"Eastern Division champion Misty faces Western Division champion Jessie to battle for the Queen of the Princess Festival title," the announcer said. "Who will be the victor?"

A bell rang. Jessie threw out a Poké Ball.

Arbok appeared. This Poison Pokémon looked like a large snake — a cobra.

Misty knew Arbok was tough to beat.

"Pikachu! Go!" Misty cried.

"Misty's opening the battle with Pikachu," said the announcer. "But Arbok may have the advantage."

"*May* have?" Jessie said. "Arbok, Wrap!"

Arbok slid across the field.

It wrapped its long purple body around Pikachu. Then Arbok started to squeeze the small Pokémon tightly.

Misty had to think fast.

She had to save Pikachu!

7

Lickitung's Attack

"Pikachu, Thunder Bolt!"

"Pika chuuuuuuuuuu!" Pikachu built up a powerful electric charge in its body. Then the charge exploded in a mighty blast.

The Thunder Bolt coursed through Arbok's body. The Poison Pokémon fainted.

The crowd cheered.

Jessie scowled. She threw out a Poké Ball. "Weezing, get that Pikachu!"

Weezing appeared. Another Poison Pokémon, Weezing looked like a black cloud with two heads.

Weezing floated through the air, ready to cover Pikachu with poison.

Pikachu didn't give it the chance. It hurled another Electric Attack at Weezing.

Weezing fainted.

The crowd cheered again.

"That was a lucky shot," Jessie said. She turned to Meowth. "Get in there, Meowth."

Meowth nodded. It ran out onto the field and charged at Pikachu, yelling, "Meowth can handle anything . . ."

Pikachu countered with another blast of electricity.

" . . . except a Thunder Shock from Pikachu!" Meowth said, dazed. The Pokémon fainted.

Misty jumped up and down. She was going to win!

"It looks like this battle is over," said the announcer.

Jessie was stunned. "I can't believe it," she said.

Meowth lifted its head up from the field. "You still have one more Pokémon, Jess," it said weakly. "Don't forget that Lickitung you caught to give to the Boss."

"That's right," Jessie said. "I have one Pokémon left!"

Jessie took out another Poké Ball and tossed it.

"Lickitung, go!" she cried.

Misty stopped jumping up and down. The Lickitung sat on the field. The pink Normal Pokémon was almost four feet tall. It looked kind of like a hippopotamus, but it had a huge tongue.

In the stands, Ash looked up the Pokémon on his Pokédex.

"Lickitung, the licking Pokémon," the Pokédex said. "It uses a tongue that is more than twice the length of its body to battle, as well as to capture food."

Misty heard.

"Pikachu, be careful and make sure that Pokémon doesn't give you a tongue lashing!" she called out.

Pikachu nodded.

"You can lick Pikachu, Lickitung!" Jessie said. "Go!"

"Pikachu, use your Thunder Bolt!" Misty commanded.

Pikachu ran up to Lickitung. Sparks flew from Pikachu's cheeks.

But before Pikachu could attack, Lickitung's mouth opened up. Its pink tongue slid out and licked Pikachu right in the face!

Pikachu grimaced. Lickitung's tongue was so gross that it made Pikachu dizzy.

Then Pikachu fainted!

"Lickitung is leading Jessie to a major upset!" the announcer cried.

Misty couldn't believe it. How could she come so far, only to be defeated by a pink Pokémon with a disgusting tongue?

She wasn't going to lose those Princess dolls.

She still had three Pokémon left.

"Misty!" Ash called out. "Use Bulbasaur. Its Vine Whip can block Lickitung's Tongue Attack."

Misty nodded. "Right, Ash! Bulbasaur, go!"

Bulbasaur charged out onto the field. Two vines lashed out of the plant bulb on its back.

But Lickitung's tongue was quicker. The

Pokémon's tongue shot out and wrapped around the vines. Then the tongue licked Bulbasaur, picked up the Grass Pokémon, and threw it across the field.

Bulbasaur was out.

Misty tried to think. What could stop Lickitung's tongue?

"Vulpix, go!" she cried. "And use your Flamethrower!"

Vulpix ran out, ready to pummel Lickitung with a stream of flame.

But once again, Lickitung was quicker. It licked Vulpix before it could attack.

Like Pikachu, Vulpix became dizzy. The Fire Pokémon reeled back and forth, and then fainted.

Now it was Jessie's turn to jump up and

down. James and Meowth cheered for her.

"This could be one of the greatest comebacks in Pokémon history!" the announcer blared. "Now Misty has only one Pokémon left to try to stop this Lickitung, or Jessie will be Queen of the Princess Festival!"

"I refuse to lose," Misty said. "So Starmie — it's up to you."

Misty tossed out another Poké Ball.

But Starmie didn't burst from the ball.

Instead, a Pokémon that looked like a yellow duck appeared.

Psyduck!

Misty groaned. *Not Psyduck!* She hung her head.

There's no way I can win now, she thought. *I might as well give up.*

Jessie laughed. "It's kind of disappointing to beat such a pathetic Pokémon," she said. "But a win's a win. Lickitung, slurp that Psyduck and let's get going!"

Lickitung gave Psyduck a wet, sticky lick with its tongue.

Psyduck didn't seem to notice.

"This is incredible!" the announcer said. "Lickitung's Lick Attack isn't working against Psyduck!"

"Lickitung, finish it off!" Jessie said angrily.

Lickitung kept licking Psyduck. It wrapped its tongue around the Pokémon.

Psyduck didn't faint. Instead, the Pokémon closed its eyes and grabbed its head.

"Something's happening," said the announcer. "Psyduck doesn't look too happy. It looks like it has a headache."

"Misty," Ash called out. "You know what happens when Psyduck gets a headache!"

Misty brightened. "That's it!" she cried. "Psychic power! Psyduck, use your Confusion Attack!"

Psyduck opened its eyes and stared at Lickitung. Lickitung began to glow with an eerie blue light. Its tongue snapped back into its mouth. The force sent Lickitung rolling down the field like a bowling ball.

Lickitung crashed into Jessie, James, and Meowth, sending Team Rocket flying out of the stadium.

"Looks like Team Rocket's blasting off again!" they cried.

"It's over! Misty wins!" the announcer said excitedly. "Misty is our new Princess Festival Queen."

Misty hugged Psyduck, Pikachu, Bulbasaur, and Vulpix. Ash and Brock ran out onto the field to congratulate her.

"Good job, Misty," Brock said.

"Yeah, you did it," Ash said. "I bet you can't wait to play with those dolls."

"Play with them? No way," Misty replied. "I'm shipping them back to my sisters in Cerulean City."

"What?" Ash asked.

"That's right," Misty said. "Then they'll finally know that I'm just as good as they are."

8

Home Again

Imagining her sisters' faces when they opened those Pokémon dolls she sent them kept Misty happy for a while. But after she was back on the road for a few weeks, she soon forgot about Lily, Daisy, and Violet. She was having too many adventures with Ash, Brock, and Pikachu.

Their travels led them back to the entrance to Viridian City. Ash was intent on earning an Earth Badge there.

The friends rested at the city gates. There was a large public fountain nearby, and Misty let out her Water Pokémon so they could swim.

Starmie and Staryu swam happily. But Horsea could barely paddle around. The Pokémon's normal blue color looked pale.

Misty looked at Horsea with concern.

"Horsea doesn't look well," she told Ash and Brock.

"Horsea," the Pokémon said weakly.

"Maybe it needs more exercise," Brock remarked. "It needs to swim in something bigger than a fountain once in a while."

"But we aren't near any oceans or lakes," Ash said.

"Too bad there isn't an aquarium around here," Brock added.

That gave Misty an idea. "There's a huge pool back home!" she said. "We can go there."

"Right!" Ash said. "There's a pool at the Cerulean City Gym."

"It's not far from here," Brock said. "We can make a quick trip and then Ash can come back and get his badge."

"Great!" Misty said. She ran to a pay phone and called her sisters.

Misty was lost in thought as the friends walked down the road to Cerulean City.

The last time Misty had gone back home, she had been afraid to see her sisters. Afraid they would think she was a loser.

But not now. She was much more experienced as a Pokémon trainer this time. And since winning the Princess Festival, she had a lot more confidence.

Who knows? Misty thought. *Maybe this visit will be fun. And besides, I can make sure my doll set arrived — and show it off.*

"Hey, look at that," Ash said.

Misty looked up. A huge billboard loomed in front of the Cerulean City Gym.

The billboard showed a painting of a red-haired mermaid swimming in the ocean. She was surrounded by Water Pokémon.

"'Come to the Underwater Ballet,'" Ash read. "'See a famous underwater star in her glorious return to Cerulean City.'"

"Cool!" Misty said. "I wonder who she is?"

"It's funny," Ash said. "She looks kind of like you."

The friends walked into the gym. Violet, Lily, and Daisy were waiting for them.

Misty's sisters ran up to her and hugged her.

"What took you so long?" Violet asked.

"We were worried about you!" Lily said.

"We're so glad you're here!" added Daisy.

"Huh?" Misty asked. She wasn't used to such a warm welcome.

"Hey, remember me?" Ash asked.

"Sure," the sisters said.

"And, uh, I'm Brock," Brock said, blushing like he always did when he was around pretty girls. "I can't wait to see your show! Has that famous underwater ballerina arrived yet? I'd love to meet her."

Lily smiled. "You already have."

Misty, Brock, and Ash looked at one another, confused.

"She just got here," Violet said.

Daisy waved her arm at Misty. "Presenting Misty, the star of the underwater ballet, *The Magical Mermaid.*"

Misty stepped back, shocked. "Me? The star?"

"You have to help us," Lily pleaded. "We're not pulling in the big crowds like we used to."

"We decided to try something new," Violet said. "This ballet will be *under*water."

"And a new star will help draw in the crowds," Daisy said. "We need you, Misty!"

"Yeah," Lily said. "Like, when we found out you won those Pokémon dolls, we knew you could handle anything."

Misty folded her arms. "This is crazy. You should have asked me first!"

"It's too late," Lily said quickly. "We already sold the tickets."

"Please, Misty," Violet said. "Do it for the sake of the gym."

Misty was silent.

"Give it a shot, Misty," Ash said.

"You can do it," Brock encouraged her.

Misty sighed. How could she argue with five people?

"Okay," Misty said. "I'll do it. Meet the new Magical Mermaid!"

9

The Misty Mermaid

"Ladies and gentlemen, our underwater ballet, *The Magical Mermaid*, performed by the exciting and talented Cerulean City Sensational Sisters, is about to begin!"

Daisy's voice blared through the gym. Every seat in the stands was filled. The crowd clapped and cheered as the lights dimmed.

A bright light shone on the pool in the center of the gym. The pool began to rise from the ground. The crowd gasped as the pool became a giant aquarium tank. Now the audience could see everything under-water perfectly.

A spotlight shone inside the tank to reveal a large group of Water Pokémon. Seel reclined on a rock. Horsea swam around, looking happy and healthy. Starmie and Staryu danced in the water, their jewels shining brightly. And a school of Goldeen swam in circles, led by a Seaking, the evolved form of Goldeen.

Then a spotlight shone on the top of the tank. A beautiful girl in a mermaid costume sat there and waved.

Misty!

I can't believe I'm doing this, Misty thought as she looked out into the gym.

Swimming underwater wasn't easy. She'd have to hold her breath for a long time. If she messed up, it would be more than embarrassing — it could be danger-ous.

Still, rehearsal had gone pretty smooth-ly. Misty the mermaid would swim with the Water Pokémon. Then Lily and Violet, dressed as villains, would come out and capture her. Daisy, dressed as a prince, would battle them for a while. She'd save Misty, and the show would be over.

Misty took a deep breath. She dove into the water.

Seel extended a fin and Misty grabbed it. They swam together in an underwater dance. The other Water Pokémon swirled around them.

Daisy narrated the story. "Once upon a time there lived a magical mermaid. She

spent many playful hours with her happy Water Pokémon."

When Misty's lungs felt like they would burst, she swam into a special cave that her sisters had designed. There was a special part of the cave that wasn't in the water. The audience couldn't see it. Misty caught her breath there, then swam back out into the water.

"The Magical Mermaid's Water Pokémon all lived their lives in peace and harmony," Daisy said. "Until one day two terrible villains appeared."

That was Misty's cue to swim into a fake giant clamshell and wait for Lily and Violet to appear. Inside the shell was a special mouthpiece that was attached to a band around her head. The mouthpiece enabled Misty to breathe — and talk — if she needed to.

Misty took a breath and looked up at the top of the tank. Now Lily and Violet were supposed to dive in. But Lily and Violet weren't standing there.

It was Jessie, James, and Meowth. They

were all dressed in silly costumes. Jessie was dressed up like a prince in a fairy tale. And James wore the gown and crown of a princess!

"It was easy getting those two silly girls out of the way," Jessie said.

"Now we can steal the show," James added.

"And steal some Water Pokémon!" finished Meowth.

Misty gasped.

From the stands, Ash and Brock recognized Team Rocket.

"We'd better go stop them!" Ash said. They ran backstage, with Pikachu right behind them.

Jessie and James put on the same special mouthpieces that Misty wore. They dove into the water.

Misty kept her mouthpiece in. She'd need air if she was going to have to battle Team Rocket.

Misty swam up to them. "What are you guys doing here?" she asked.

"We're staging a grand finale," Jessie said. "Look!"

Misty looked up. Team Rocket's hot-air balloon came crashing down through the gym's ceiling. Meowth was at the helm.

"Bring up all those Water Pokémon and we'll bring down the house!" Meowth said. The Pokémon lowered a large net into the water tank. All the Water Pokémon quickly got tangled in the net.

Angry, Misty grabbed the edge of the net. "You can't steal these Pokémon. Let go!"

"Make like a clam and scram!" James snapped.

Jessie and James grabbed the net. They tried to pull it away from Misty.

The crowd clapped. They didn't know it

was real. They thought the fight was part of the show.

Daisy didn't know Misty was in trouble, either. "When it looked like all was lost," she announced, "a charming and handsome prince arrived to save the day."

Misty heard a loud splash. She looked up. Ash, Brock, and Pikachu swam into the tank. All three wore special mouthpieces connected to air tanks.

James scowled. "It's *those twerps* again. We'll show them!"

Jessie threw out a Poké Ball. "Arbok, go!"
The Poison Pokémon swam out.

"Go, Horsea!" Misty called.

Arbok and Horsea charged at each other. Horsea squirted bubbles from its snout. The fast bubbles zoomed toward Arbok.

But Arbok used its strong tail to hit the bubbles right back at Horsea.

Then the Poison Pokémon began to wrap its body around Horsea, strangling it!

10

The Big Finish

"Horsea! Smoke Screen!" Misty commanded.

A burst of smoke shot from Horsea's snout. Confused, Arbok lost its grip.

At the same time, Seaking swam swiftly through the smoke. It used the sharp horn on its head to jab Arbok.

"Seaking! Horn Drill!" Misty ordered.

Seaking's horn began to spin like a drill. The Water Pokémon lunged at Arbok, attacking it with the drill.

James decided to give Arbok some help.

"Weezing, go!" James shouted. He threw a Poké Ball.

The two-headed Pokémon appeared. But Weezing couldn't breathe underwater. It coughed and swam to the top of the tank.

Ash threw a Poké Ball next. "Squirtle! I choose you!"

Squirtle, a Water Pokémon that looked like a cute turtle, appeared.

"Underwater Tackle!" Ash commanded.

"Good idea," Misty said. "Seaking, Starmie, Tackle!"

Squirtle, Seaking, and Starmie all attacked Arbok at once. But the strong Pokémon quickly recovered from the tackles.

"Arbok, Poison Sting, now!" Jessie commanded.

Arbok rose up. It lashed its tail back and forth. Then it bared its fangs.

Misty was worried. One bite from Arbok would deliver a powerful dose of poison. No Water Pokémon could defeat that.

But before Arbok could take a bite out of any of them, Seel swam between them.

James just laughed. "That little baby actually thinks it can stop us!"

"Finish it off, Arbok!" Jessie said.

Seel bravely swam in circles around Arbok, creating a whirlpool. Arbok grew dizzy.

"Good work, Seel!" Misty shouted. "Headbutt now!"

Seel charged at Arbok and rammed into it with the horn on top of its head.

"Seel! Aurora Beam!" Misty commanded.

Seel's horn began to spin. A rainbow-colored beam shone from the horn. The beam hit Arbok.

"Chaaaaaaaaa!" the snakelike Pokémon cried.

Arbok was weakened.

Misty was so proud of the Water Pokémon. The crowd roared.

Then something strange happened to Seel. The Pokémon began to glow with light. The white light filled the pool. Then it dimmed.

Seel was gone. In its place was a bigger and stronger Pokémon with a long tail.

"It's Dewgong!" Misty cried.

Seel had evolved!

The crowd went wild.

Jessie was impatient. "Okay, Arbok," she said. "Get that Seel or Doodad or whatever it is."

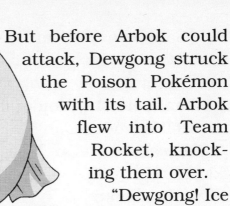

But before Arbok could attack, Dewgong struck the Poison Pokémon with its tail. Arbok flew into Team Rocket, knocking them over.

"Dewgong! Ice Beam!" Misty cried.

Dewgong sent out another beam from the horn on its head. The beam hit Arbok, Jessie, and James.

And trapped them in ice!

Meowth quickly scooped up its frozen friends in the net hanging from their hot-air balloon. Then the balloon flew away.

"It looks like the show's over for Team Rocket!" Meowth cried.

Misty, Ash, Brock, Pikachu, and the other Pokémon left the pool and stood on the edge of the tank.

The audience cheered and clapped as they all took a bow.

Backstage, Misty's sisters hugged her.

"Thanks to you, our shows are totally sold out for the next six months," Daisy said.

"Can you stay and play the mermaid?" Violet asked. "We'd really like it if you could."

Misty looked at her sisters. It felt good knowing that they wanted her to join them. They didn't think she was a little pipsqueak anymore.

Then she looked at Ash, Brock, and Pikachu. Her best friends. If it weren't for her adventures with them, Misty never would have learned to be a good trainer.

Besides, catching Pokémon was a lot more fun than swimming around in a silly mermaid costume.

"I'm going to get back on the road," Misty said.

Lily smiled. "That's okay. Violet and I will take turns playing the mermaid. But we'll miss you!"

Misty hugged her sisters. "I'll miss you, too. Take good care of my Princess dolls. I'll be back for them someday."

"We will," her sisters replied.

"So, what are we waiting for?" Ash asked impatiently. "Let's get going. I'll never become the World's Greatest Pokémon Master standing around here all day."

"Give me a break," Misty snapped. "I could stand around all day and still be a better trainer than you."

"Oh, yeah?" Ash faced Misty angrily.

"Hey, you two," Brock interrupted. "Do you think you could stop fighting just for one day?"

"I guess so," Ash said.

Misty looked at Ash. She smiled. "Sure," she said.

She could manage not to argue with Ash today.

After all, there was always tomorrow!

POKéMON

now on video everywhere!

14⁹⁸ each

five volumes available:

...Choose You! Pikachu!

...ystery of Mt. Moon

...ters of Cerulean City

Poké-Friends

Thunder Shock

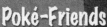 more info see **www.pioneeranimation.com**